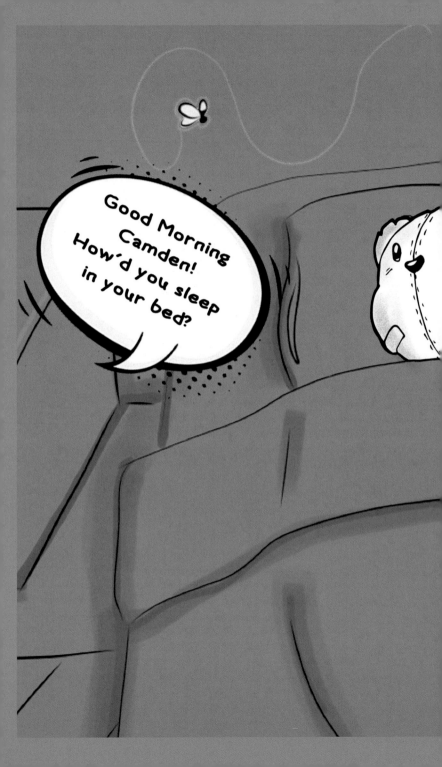

What began with a collection of t-shirts has grown into an entire movement, trying to redefine American style and perception. My Heart BeatZ has always stood for providing quality products, creating worlds and inviting people to take part in their dream. We try to be innovators of lifestyle advertisements that tell a story of the Dreamers & Believers and the first to create stores that encourage customers to participate in that lifestyle.

My Heart BeatZ takes this participation to a new level as a rich and exciting interactive destination. When you're transported into the world of My Heart BeatZ online, you can shop for great products for yourself and your home, and also learn about adventure, style and culture on MHB TV.

"Back when all this started, I felt sure that there were no boundaries. I'm even more sure of that today." -EP

Made in the USA
Monee, IL
12 October 2022

15754448R00017